W9-AAX-352

Helaine Becker   Orbie

SLOTH

at the
Zoom

ZzZzZOO

zoom

ZOO
ANIMAL TRANSPORT

Owlkids Books

One bright day, a truck whizzed up to the front gate of the Zoom. There was a new animal being delivered.

It was a sloth.

DELIVERY

Deliver to
Zzzzzoo
37 Zoo Street

It took a long time for the zoomkeepers
to get the sloth out of the truck.

First they had
to wake her up.

Then she needed
a sip of water...

and a bit of a
stretch, too.

When she finally looked around,
the sloth was perplexed.
You see, she thought her new
home would be pretty laid-back.

But this was the Zoom, not the Zzzzzoo.

At the Zoom, the zebras galloped so fast they left their stripes in puddles.

The monkeys climbed so
fast they forgot to stop
at the treetops.

And the parrots flew so
fast their tails drew
rainbows across the sky.

What's all this
fuss and flutter
about?

wondered
the sloth.

After a few weeks, the sloth was ready to make a new friend.

Can't stop now!

the monkeys screeched.

We're running ever so late!

They raced up and down and round and round the jungle gym.

The sloth shrugged her shaggy shoulders.
Then she chose a comfy spot where the
sun's golden rays would tickle her belly
all day long.

A few weeks after that, the sloth flagged down the zebras as they zipped by.

I like...

. . .your stripes,

she called.

They whinnied their thanks
without stopping.

The sloth sighed.
She shook her shaggy head.

No one here
has any time.

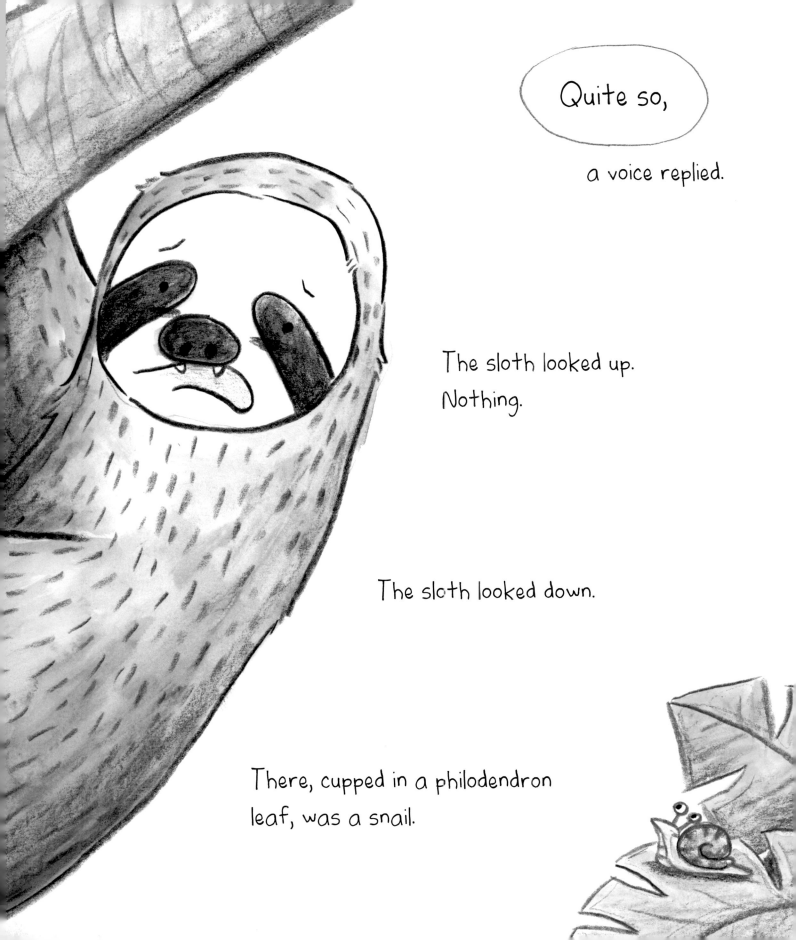

Quite so,

a voice replied.

The sloth looked up.
Nothing.

The sloth looked down.

There, cupped in a philodendron leaf, was a snail.

"Why. . ."

"hello down there," said the sloth.

"Nice to meet you."

There was a long silence.

Then the snail said,

"Since you don't seem too busy. . ."

"perhaps you'd care to have a snack. . ."

"with me?"

There was another long, comfortable pause.

When the sloth arrived at the snail's leaf, they shared a bite.

Then they shared a cool drink.

And as the setting sun
adorned the sky, they
shared a contented sigh.

The monkeys swung over.

What are you doing?

Sloth offered them some iced tea.

Next came the cheetah.

What's going on?

Snail offered her a sweet, green leaf to nibble on.

Mind if we join you?

asked the zebras.

Everyone shuffled to make some room.

And as day became night
and night became day, the animals
at the Zoom slowed down...

. . .just long enough, that is, to become fast friends.

For the world's slowpokes, dawdlers and lazybones.
Go ahead—take another nap. —HB

For my two favorite little monkeys. For all our crazy
(and lazy) moments. —O

Text © 2018 Helaine Becker
Illustrations © 2018 Orbie

All rights reserved. No part of this publication may be reproduced, stored in a retrieval system, or transmitted in
any form or by any means, without the prior written permission of Owlkids Books Inc., or in the case of photocopying
or other reprographic copying, a license from the Canadian Copyright Licensing Agency (Access Copyright). For an
Access Copyright license, visit www.accesscopyright.ca or call toll-free to 1-800-893-5777.

Owlkids Books acknowledges the financial support of the Canada Council for the Arts, the Ontario Arts Council, the
Government of Canada through the Canada Book Fund (CBF) and the Government of Ontario through the Ontario
Media Development Corporation's Book Initiative for our publishing activities.

Published in Canada by
Owlkids Books Inc.
10 Lower Spadina Avenue
Toronto, ON M5V 2Z2

Published in the United States by
Owlkids Books Inc.
1700 Fourth Street
Berkeley, CA 94710

Library and Archives Canada Cataloguing in Publication

Becker, Helaine, 1961-, author
    Sloth at the zoom / Helaine Becker ; illustrated by Orbie.

ISBN 978-1-77147-249-4 (hardcover)

    I. Orbie, 1984-, illustrator II. Title.

PS8553.E295532S66 2018   jC813'.6   C2017-907425-3

Library of Congress Control Number: 2017961368

Edited by Jennifer MacKinnon
Designed by Danielle Arbour and Alisa Baldwin

ONTARIO ARTS COUNCIL
CONSEIL DES ARTS DE L'ONTARIO
an Ontario government agency
un organisme du gouvernement de l'Ontario

Canada Council
for the Arts

Conseil des Arts
du Canada

Canadä

Manufactured in Shenzhen, Guangdong, China, in March 2018, by WKT Co. Ltd.
Job #17CB2758

A   B   C   D   E   F

Publisher of Chirp, chickaDEE and OWL
www.owlkidsbooks.com

Owlkids Books is a division of

Bayard
CANADA